silly Millies

Ugh! A Bug!

Ned Crowley

Millbrook Press   Minneapolis

Cover photograph courtesy of Animals Animals (© Bill Beatty)

Photographs courtesy of Animals Animals: pp. 1 (© Patti Murray),
3 (© Zig Lesczynski), 4 (© Patti Murray), 5 (bottom © Stephen Dalton),
6 (© Bill Beatty), 8 (© James H. Robinson), 9 (© Michael Fogden),
10 (© Stephen Dalton), 11 (© ABPL Image Library), 12–13 (bottom © Michael
Fogden), 14 (top © Michael Fogden), 14 (bottom © Michael Fogden/OSF),
15 (© G. I. Bernard/OSF), 17 (© Color-Pic), 18 (© Fabio Colombini Medeiros),
19 (© Michael Fogden/OSF), 20 (© Jack De Coningh), 22 (© Jorg & Petra
Wegner), 23 (© Richard Laval), 24 (© Joyce & Paul Berquist), 25
(© John Anderson), 26–27 (© Patti Murray), 29 (© Patti Murray);
Photo Researchers, Inc.: pp. 5 (top © M. H. Sharp), 16 (© Wayne Lawler),
21 (© L. & D. Klein); Peter Arnold, Inc.: p. 7 (© S. J. Krasemann);
Nature's Faces: p. 12–13 (top © Parvis M. Pour)

Millbrook Press
A division of Lerner Publishing Group
241 First Avenue North
Minneapolis, Minnesota 55401 U.S.A.

Website address: www.lernerbooks.com

Library of Congress Cataloging-in-Publication Data

Crowley, Ned.
    Ugh! : a bug! / written by Ned Crowley.
       p.   cm. — (Silly Millies)
    Summary: Illustrations and simple text describe some unusual characteristics of
such insects as grasshoppers, beetles, caterpillars, praying mantis, and more.
    ISBN-13: 978–0-7613-3450-7 (lib. bdg.)
    ISBN-10: 0-7613-3450-5 (lib. bdg.)
    [1. Insects—Fiction.]   I. Title. II. Series.
PZ7.C88765Ug 2006   [E]-dc22   2003017948

Manufactured in the United States of America
1 2 3 4 5 6 – DP – 11 10 09 08 07 06

Or not
at all?

Or did it dig?

. . . or twig?

15

What is a Bug?

To be a true bug, you need two things. You need a mouth that pierces and sucks, and you need two sets of wings. One set is hard. The other set is soft. A ladybug is a bug. Some of the creatures in this book are not really bugs. They are insects. Insects don't always have the two things needed to be a bug. So—all bugs are insects, but not all insects are bugs.

Did you Know?

There are more insects on Earth than any other animal.

Insects have a chain of small hearts to pump blood around their bodies.

Flies can taste with their feet.

A dragonfly can fly as fast as 30 miles per hour.

A Little Secret . . .

Remember the caterpillar at the beginning and end of this book?
That is not really its face. It is its bottom! Its real face is on the other end. Scientists think this fake face makes the caterpillars look scary to birds. What do you think?

The Bugs in this Book

Page 1
Giraffe-necked Beetle

Page 8
Pill Bug

Pages 3, 4, 26, 27, 29
Spicebush Swallowtail
Butterfly Caterpillar

Page 9
Spiny Bug

Page 5
Florida Leaf-footed Bug

Page 10
Short-horned Grasshopper

Page 5
Grasshopper

Page 11
Tenebnonid Beetle

Page 6
Dogday Harvestfly

Page 12
Nebraska Cone-head
Grasshopper

Page 7
Assassin Bug

Page 13
Praying Mantis

Page 14
Atlas Moth

Page 14
Snouth Beetle

Page 15
Millipede

Page 16
Eupholus Weevil

Page 17
Goliath Beetle

Page 18
Long Horn Beetle

Page 19
Spike-headed Katydid

Page 20
A pair of weevils

Page 21
Colombian Cone-headed
Grasshopper

Page 22
Cockchafer Beetle

Page 23
Rainforest Katydid

Page 24
Praying Mantis

Page 25
S. E. Lubber
Grasshopper

About the Author

Ned Crowley is the author of several children's books including *NaNook & Pryce*, *Aliens Took My Daughter*, and *What's Behind the Bump?*, the last of which he illustrated. Ned's interest in bugs began when someone offered him a nickel to eat one—and he accepted!

In his spare time, Ned works full time in advertising, writing and producing lots of television commercials. He currently lives in Chicago with his wife, Karen, and their three daughters, Shea, Robyn, and Grace.

Tips for Discussion

- Insects look the way they do for a reason. Can you guess why a bug might need long legs, or be green like a leaf, or have a hard shell?

- Have fun designing your own bug. What colors would it be? What kind of eyes? Would it have wings or lots of legs? What silly name could you call your bug?

- Insects can sometimes seem scary, but can you think of ways that insects help us? Name some animals that depend on bugs for food. Why do plants need bugs too?